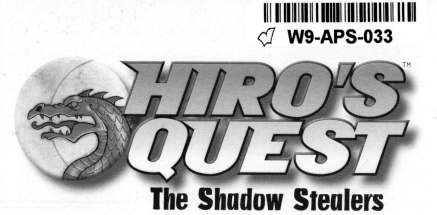

HIRO'S QUEST™
The Shadow Stealers

by Tracey West

Illustrated by Craig Phillips

Scholastic Inc.

**New York   Toronto   London   Auckland
Sydney   Mexico City   New Delhi   Hong Kong**

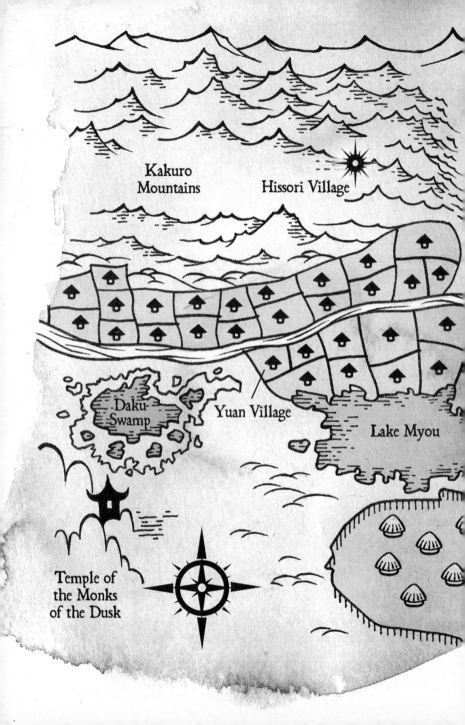

Kagetsu
Mountains

Washi Plain

Forest of
the Yosei

Karibi

Okibi

Hebi River

**Herutsu Province
in the Kingdom of Kenkoro**

For Will, Shannon, and Zane,
who would all make great ninja.
— T. W.

ISBN 978-0-545-20100-1

12 11 10 9 8 7 6 5 4 3 2 1   10 11 12 13 14 15/0

Printed in the U.S.A.   40
First printing, May 2010
Book design by Jennifer Rinaldi Windau

Chapter One

Three ninja marched up the steep mountain path.

"What kind of mission are we going on, exactly?" Hiro Hinata called ahead to his brothers, Kenta and Kazuki.

Kenta laughed. "I wouldn't exactly call it a mission, Hiro. It's just a little old lady with a big imagination."

"You mean Mrs. Sasaki?" Hiro asked. "She's not so little."

"It's a waste of time," Kazuki grumbled. "Missing chickens. She's probably got a brain full of feathers."

The three brothers were dressed similarly. Each one wore a tunic over loose-flowing pants and the symbol of the Hinata family around his neck: a metal disk engraved with a sun and moon entwined.

Other than that, the boys looked very different. Kazuki, the oldest at seventeen, was also the largest, with a broad chest and big muscles he loved to brag about. Fifteen-year-old Kenta was slim and athletic, with short, spiky blue hair. Hiro was eleven years old and the shortest one in the family so far. His wiry body was more like Kenta's than Kazuki's and his reddish brown hair flopped across his forehead.

"So Mrs. Sasaki's chickens are missing," Hiro said. "Why exactly are we going there?"

"Because if you haven't noticed, that's the job of the Hinata family," Kazuki snapped. "We assist the people of Hissori Village when there's trouble. Mom and Dad usually get to do all the good stuff. Kenta and I have been chasing chickens since we were your age."

Hiro thought about this as they continued on the path. He'd gone on his first ninja mission a few weeks earlier, and it had been much more exciting than chasing chickens. His family, along with his friends Aya and Yoshi, had traveled far from the village to retrieve the magical Amulet of the Moon and Amulet of the Sun. They had faced a powerful ninja named Fujita, who'd wanted to use the amulets' power to rule the kingdom of Kenkoro, and Hiro had helped defeat him.

Part of him wanted to go on another exciting adventure. Then he remembered how terrifying his fight with Fujita had been. Maybe helping an old lady wasn't such a bad deal.

"Oh, there you are!" Mrs. Sasaki belted out.

The old woman wore a blue kimono over her round body, making Hiro think of a giant blueberry. She greeted Kazuki and Kenta with big hugs. Then Hiro saw she was coming for him.

"Oh, little Hiro's all grown up!" she said, gripping him tightly. Hiro gasped for breath as she released him. Then she pinched both of his cheeks, hard. "You look like your father, don't you? What a good boy."

She looked up at the brothers. "Thank you for coming. I know you will be able to help. Someone is stealing my chickens!" Her dark eyes narrowed, and her voice fell to a whisper. "I think it's an evil ninja."

"An evil ninja who likes chickens?" Kenta joked.

"Who doesn't like chickens?" Mrs. Sasaki asked. "Come, let me show you."

She led them around the back of her small house to stand in front of a fenced-in yard. Wire netting was attached to wood posts to keep the chickens inside. A few white birds strutted around the yard, pecking at the dirt. Others sat inside the shade of the chicken coop.

"Mystery solved!" Kazuki said. He turned around. "Let's go."

"Silly boy. Those are just *some* of my chickens,"

Mrs. Sasaki told him, shaking her head. "I'm missing three."

"We'll help you, Mrs. Sasaki," Hiro said. "Don't worry."

Mrs. Sasaki pinched his cheeks again. "I knew you were a good boy!" She moved around to the side of the house. "Let me get you all some cold water. It's going to be warm today."

Kazuki waited until she was gone. "This is ridiculous!" he said. "What are we supposed to do?"

"I could transform into a wolf and sniff around," Kenta suggested. Like most ninja, Kenta had the ability to transform into his animal spirit whenever he wanted to.

"That might scare the chickens," Hiro pointed out. "Let's try using our human noses first."

Hiro opened the rickety gate and walked inside the yard. The chickens strutted around him as though he wasn't there. Hiro started looking around. He wasn't sure what he was looking for—until he saw it.

There was a small hole in the wire netting at the far side of the gate. It was large enough for a chicken to pass through.

"Kenta, Kazuki, look!" Hiro said, pointing.

"Aha!" Kenta said. "Hole in fence equals missing chickens."

"So what do we do now?" Hiro asked.

"We fix it," Kazuki said. "Actually, you fix it. Kenta and I are taking a break."

"But you haven't done anything yet!" Hiro protested.

Kazuki leaned back against the fence. "I've been doing stuff like this for six years. Now it's your turn."

Kenta grinned and hopped up on one of the posts. "That's right, little brother. Now get to work!"

Hiro sighed. He knew there was no point in arguing.

Hiro found Mrs. Sasaki and explained the problem. He returned with a scrap of netting. Then he knelt down in front of the fence.

"Faster, faster, Hiro!" Kazuki ordered.

"And don't forget to tap into all your ninja skills," Kenta added. Then the two boys burst out laughing.

Hiro ignored them. He used his small fingers to weave the scrap into the rest of the net. It was tedious work.

Kazuki would never be able to do this, anyway, Hiro thought. *His fingers are too fat!*

As Hiro worked, a tiny black kitten ran up to his brothers, nuzzled Kazuki's feet, and then jumped up to nip at Kenta. Then the kitten spotted Kazuki's shadow and froze, alarmed. She eyed the shadow, standing perfectly still except for her tail, which swayed back and forth.

Pounce! The kitten attacked the shadow like a lion pouncing on her prey. Hiro smiled and turned back to the fence. A moment later, the kitten sidled up to him, nuzzling his leg.

Hiro laughed. He glanced over at his brothers.

"This kitten is so cute!" he said.

Kazuki and Kenta didn't answer. Then Hiro noticed

something strange. The sun shone down on the brothers, but Hiro didn't see their shadows anywhere. It was like the shadows had just disappeared.

He shrugged it off as some kind of trick of the light.

"Did you hear me?" Hiro said. "We should ask Mom and Dad for a kitten like this one!"

Kazuki's head slumped down on his chest.

Bam! He collapsed on the ground.

Kenta went next. He toppled off the fence post, landing in the dirt with a thud.

Hiro jumped up and raced toward his brothers.

"Kenta! Kazuki!" he cried.

Chapter Two

Hiro put his hand on Kazuki's chest. He could feel the rise and fall of his brother's breathing, but otherwise, Kazuki was motionless. Kenta was the same.

"Cut it out!" Hiro yelled. "This isn't funny!"

Mrs. Sasaki appeared behind him. "What's going on? Are your brothers sleeping on the job?"

Hiro shook his head. "I think something's wrong. One minute they were fine, and the next . . ."

Mrs. Sasaki examined the two boys and frowned.

"Hurry and get your mother and father, Hiro. I'll watch over the boys while you're gone."

Hiro hesitated. He hated to leave, but he knew he wasn't strong enough to carry either one of his brothers. He raced back to the mountain path.

Then he remembered—he knew a faster way to get home. Hiro stopped and closed his eyes.

I need some monkey speed!

The transformation happened quickly. His body got smaller while his arms grew longer and more powerful. A long tail sprouted from his lower back. Bushy gold fur covered his skin.

Hiro climbed the nearest tree and then swung from branch to branch, hurrying back to his family's home. He had learned how to transform into his spirit animal only a few weeks earlier, and each time he felt a little more comfortable in his new body.

He swung down to the ground and ran the rest of the way to his front door. A stray black cat paced in front of the open front door. Hiro jumped over the cat to get inside.

"Mom! Dad!" Hiro called out.

"In here, Hiro," responded his father, Yuto.

Hiro followed his father's voice to his parents' bedroom. His mother, Rino, lay motionless on top of the white sheets of the bed. Yuto knelt beside her, holding her hand.

"Is Mom all right?" Hiro asked.

Yuto looked worried. "She collapsed suddenly, Hiro. I am not sure why."

"The same thing has happened to Kenta and Kazuki," Hiro blurted out. "They're at Mrs. Sasaki's house. I had to leave them there while I came to get help."

Yuto stood. "This is even stranger than I thought," he said. "Watch over your mother, Hiro. I will find some men in the village to help me get your brothers back here. Then we will find Mr. Sato. He may know what this is all about."

Hiro's father swiftly left the room. Hiro sat on the edge of the bed and nervously watched over his mother, hoping every moment that she would open her eyes. His heart beat quickly in his chest. Everything was happening so fast!

He was anxious to see Mr. Sato. The old man had trained Hiro and his friends to become ninja since they were young. Then recently, when Fujita had tried to steal the amulets, they had learned Mr. Sato's secret. He was actually the legendary ninja Okuno. He had come to Hissori Village in secret, to protect the scrolls that showed the location of the amulets. Mr. Sato was the wisest ninja in the kingdom. Surely he could help Hiro's family.

Hiro heard a voice at the door.

"Hiro! Hiro! Are you okay?"

A short boy with silvery hair bounded into the room, followed by a tall, slim girl with sleek black hair. Hiro was relieved to see his friends Yoshi and Aya.

"Everyone in the village is saying that something is wrong with Kenta and Kazuki," Yoshi blurted out. He stopped when he saw Rino. "Oh, no! Your mom, too?"

"It happened so fast," Hiro said. "They just passed

out. Dad's getting Kenta and Kazuki. Then we're going to get Mr. Sato. Dad thinks he can help."

"Why wait?" Yoshi asked. He closed his eyes. His body shimmered for a moment, and in the next instant, a rabbit with silver fur hopped up and down in Yoshi's place. "Be right back!"

Aya put a cool hand on Hiro's shoulder. Her soothing, calm energy started to wash away Hiro's nerves.

"Mr. Sato will know what to do," she said confidently.

"I hope so," Hiro replied.

A few minutes later, the small house was filled with activity. Yuto returned with three men, who carried Kenta and Kazuki inside the house. Hiro and Aya helped move the boys' beds into Rino's room so that it would be easier to keep watch over all three of them.

Next, Yoshi, who had transformed back into his normal body, returned with Mr. Sato. The old man walked quickly, despite his leaning on a cane. His long beard was as white as the simple robe he wore.

He and Yuto greeted each other with bows of respect and then nodded to the three village men as they left.

"Let us have a seat at the table," Mr. Sato said. "Please explain what has happened."

"It was very fast," Yuto began. "Rino was outside painting a view of the mountains. She was telling me about a stray cat that kept sticking her paw into her paint pots. She was talking and laughing, and then she was silent. When I looked, she had fallen off of her chair."

"The same thing happened to Kenta and Kazuki," Hiro said. "They were over by the fence, and then they suddenly fell."

Mr. Sato was thoughtful for a moment. "I must be truthful," he said finally. "I do not know what has caused this."

Hiro felt disappointment crush his hopes. If Mr. Sato didn't know what to do, then all was lost.

"However," the old man continued, "it is interesting to me that Rino, Kenta, and Kazuki have all wielded

the Amulet of the Moon. Perhaps this has something to do with their condition."

Hiro considered this. The Amulet of the Moon and the Amulet of the Sun were both powerful tools of magic. The moon amulet had been created by the Gekkani family, his mother's ancestors. Rino was able to access the power of the amulet. Kenta and Kazuki, who had the same blue gray eyes as their mother, were also able to harness it.

"There is a full moon tonight," Aya pointed out. "Could that have something to do with it?"

Mr. Sato nodded. "It is possible," he said. "Perhaps the cycles of the moon have a strange effect on those who handle the amulet."

Yuto looked pale and worried. He ran a hand through his closely cropped hair.

"How can we be sure?" he asked. "What if it's something worse? What if they never wake up?"

"There are men who may know the truth," Mr. Sato told him. "The Monks of the Dusk. Their temple lies past Daku Swamp, beyond the Hebi River. If we travel there, perhaps we will find the answers we are looking for." Mr. Sato stood up. "Yuto, I suggest you stay here and watch over your family to make sure no more harm befalls them. I will have the other ninja accompany me."

Hiro, Aya, and Yoshi exchanged looks. *The other ninja.* Mr. Sato was talking about them!

"Rest well tonight," Mr. Sato told them. "We leave at sunrise."

Chapter Three

The full moon was still visible as the party set out the next morning. It hung just over the horizon, casting a pale glow over the dark blue sky.

"It's still dark out," Aya grumbled. "I thought we were leaving at sunrise."

"The sun *is* rising, Aya," Yoshi told her. "You just hate waking up."

Aya was too cranky to reply. She and Yoshi led the group, followed by Mr. Sato. Hiro walked slowly behind them, but not because he was tired. He was thinking.

The last time he had left Hissori Village, his whole family had been with him. It felt strange not to have them along. Aya and Yoshi must have felt the same way when they'd left their families behind to find the amulets. That hadn't occurred to him before.

Mr. Sato was getting way ahead of him. Hiro adjusted his pack and picked up his pace. He carried his mother's cooking pot along with his bedroll and some food for the journey. But what made the pack heavy was the knowledge that it held something of great power—the Amulet of the Moon.

Mr. Sato had insisted that Hiro be the one to carry it. Luckily, Rino kept the amulet in a small wooden box. She and Hiro's brothers were the only ones who could even touch the amulet. But the box could be carried by anyone.

"It is your family's responsibility to guard the amulets," Mr. Sato had said, handing the box to Hiro. "I know you will take good care of it."

With each step, Hiro thought of something bad that could happen to the amulet. What if it fell out of his pack? What if an animal carried it off? What if someone tried to steal it?

Aya slowed down to walk beside him. "You look worried, Hiro. I can always tell. You get a funny look in your eyes."

Hiro smiled at her. It was nice of Aya to notice.

"I'm worried about Mom and Kenta and Kazuki, I guess," he said. "And the amulet. I don't think Fujita is strong enough to try to get it. At least, Mr. Sato says he isn't. But what if he's wrong?"

"You beat Fujita once before," Aya pointed out. "If you have to, you'll beat him again."

Talking with Aya always made Hiro feel better. His pack didn't seem so heavy anymore. The sun was brighter now, too, and slowly burned off the morning chill.

Hiro's village was one of many small villages nestled in the Kakuro Mountains. Mr. Sato knew his way around the winding foothills of the mountains. Their path was hilly, but never too steep.

Hiro, Aya, and Yoshi passed the time by joking around and telling stories. The hours went quickly. The travelers left the foothills just as the sun began to set over the mountain peaks behind them. They entered a wide expanse of farmland. Green fields stretched as far as Hiro could see.

"This valley leads to the Hebi River," Mr. Sato announced. "Let us find a place to set up camp. I am not as young as I used to be, and a rest would be good."

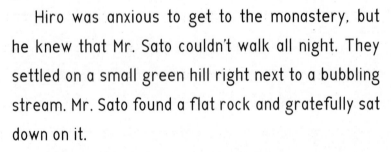

Hiro was anxious to get to the monastery, but he knew that Mr. Sato couldn't walk all night. They settled on a small green hill right next to a bubbling stream. Mr. Sato found a flat rock and gratefully sat down on it.

"This will do," he said. He pointed at the stream with his cane. "This stream will lead us to the river. I know a ferryman who can take us across. We will continue on our journey in the morning. But first, we eat."

"I can cook some rice," Aya offered.

"I'll help," Hiro said. "Yoshi, can you make a fire?"

Yoshi nodded. "One fire, coming right up!"

While Mr. Sato rested, the three friends made supper. Aya and Hiro cooked the rice and then added some small dried fish, which became fragrant and flavorful in the hot steam. After eating, they washed their bowls in the stream before it got dark. Then they returned to the fire and set up their bedrolls.

"We will sleep soon," Mr. Sato said. "But first, your training. We have not had a proper training session in a long while."

Yoshi yawned. "Training? Now?"

"A ninja is always training," Mr. Sato told him. "And this session will not be difficult. To participate, all you must do is listen."

"We're talking about Yoshi, remember?" Aya said, teasing.

"Then you must also focus," Mr. Sato added. He began to tap a point in the center of his forehead.

"What are you doing?" Hiro asked.

"I am activating one of the most powerful tools a ninja possesses," Mr. Sato said. "It is helpful if you

encounter an enemy who uses magic."

"Like Fujita," Hiro said.

"Correct," said Mr. Sato. "Not all of your enemies will be ninja. Some may be sorcerers. And some, like Fujita, may be both. They will use magic against you. But if you can see where it is coming from, you can better find a way to fight it."

Yoshi started tapping his forehead. "So doing this will help me see magic? I feel kind of silly."

"You should not care about looking silly," Mr. Sato said. "This motion opens up a channel to the pineal gland inside the body. This gland enables you to see what your eyes cannot see."

Hiro began to tap his forehead. He didn't feel any different. Apparently, neither did Yoshi or Aya. The three of them waited in silence for something to happen.

After what seemed like a very long time, Mr. Sato spoke up. "There is no magic in the field tonight," he said. "Except the magic of sleep. Good night."

Soon their teacher was snoring peacefully. Hiro

climbed into his bedroll.

"Does anyone else think that was weird?" Yoshi whispered.

"A little," Hiro admitted.

"Maybe Mr. Sato's just tired," Aya added.

Hiro yawned. "Me, too," he said. He closed his eyes and rolled over onto his side.

Aaaaaiiiiiooooowwww!

Hiro's eyes snapped open.

"What was that?" he asked in a harsh whisper.

"Sounded like a cat," Yoshi said.

"Out here?" Hiro asked.

"This is farmland," Aya reminded him. "Where there are mice, there are cats."

Hiro yawned. "You're right," he said. "Good night."

Then he fell into a deep sleep.

Chapter Four

They all woke early the next morning and ate a breakfast of bread, cheese made from the milk of Yoshi's family's goats, and clear, cold water from the stream. Then they packed up camp, doused the remains of the fire, and followed the stream to the Hebi River.

It was almost noon when the river dock came into view. Hiro pointed to a wide, flat boat bobbing up and down on the water.

"We're here!" Hiro cried. He broke into a run.

A tall, thin man in a gray tunic and pants stood next to the boat. He bowed when they approached. "I am Mr. Miyake," the ferryman told them.

They bowed back. Mr. Sato introduced himself.

"And these are my companions," he said, pointing to Hiro, Aya, and Yoshi. Then he pressed some coins into Mr. Miyake's hands. "We would be grateful for passage across the river."

They climbed across the wide, flat boat. A cool, slow breeze blew across the calm surface of the river as they glided across the water. Mr. Miyake steered with one long oar.

"How far is it to the monastery once we get across?" Hiro asked.

"There is an inn in the village of Yuan that I hope to reach before nightfall," Mr. Sato said. "The monastery is not too far from there."

Hiro frowned. "You mean we won't get to the monastery today?" Even though it was exciting to be on a journey with his friends, he still worried about his mom and brothers. The sooner they got to the monastery, the sooner he could help them.

"Daku Swamp is a dangerous place," Mr. Sato replied. "Crossing at night would not be wise."

Hiro started to ask what was dangerous about the swamp, but changed his mind. He had enough to worry about already.

"Patience, Hiro," Mr. Sato said with kindness in his voice. "I believe your mother and brothers will be safe until we return."

The words comforted Hiro.

"Thanks," he said.

The journey across the river didn't take long. When they reached the other side, they found a family of farmers waiting to make the return trip. The farmer's wife wore a wide-brimmed hat and carried a cage with three white chickens inside. Hiro thought of Mrs. Sasaki and smiled.

They walked for the rest of the day, passing through several villages. The closer they got to the swamp, the smaller and emptier the villages became.

The setting sun found them walking down a stone path. It led them to a small village square that boasted a horse stable, a market, and a two-story wood building with a sign over the door that simply read INN.

"This is where we will spend the night," Mr. Sato said.

He pushed open the door to reveal a dimly lit room with a few tables and chairs arranged in front of an empty fireplace. A man with thinning gray hair sat behind a desk in the corner. He raised an eyebrow when he saw them.

"Visitors?" he asked. "Now, that's a sight. Where are you folks headed?"

"We're going to the—" Hiro began, but Mr. Sato put a hand in front of him.

"Just passing through," Mr. Sato said pleasantly. "Do you have a room for us tonight?"

The man stood up. "Every room in the house!" he said, opening his arms wide. "Take your pick. I've got a nice big room with four beds if you and your kids want to stick together."

Hiro started to giggle, and he heard Yoshi holding his breath behind him. The thought of them all being a family was kind of funny.

"That will be fine," Mr. Sato replied. "Thank you."

"Do you have any food?" Yoshi asked, rubbing his stomach.

The man shook his head. "We had to close the kitchen a few years ago. Strangest thing. When I was a boy, the swamp was far away from here. Now it's practically at our door. Some folks say it's a living thing, growing every year." Then he remembered the question. "I have some rice I can share with you. But if you knock on the back door of the market down the road, they may open it for you. They've got fresh vegetables there, and Mrs. Tanaka makes a good chicken soup."

Yoshi licked his lips. "I could go for a carrot."

Mr. Sato nodded to them. "I will retire to the room. When you are done at the market, please come right back."

"Don't worry, Mr. Sato," Yoshi said. "If we meet any robbers, we'll take care of them!"

The innkeeper chuckled. "You won't find any robbers around here. Nothing exciting ever happens in this village."

The night was dark, and the moon shone low in the sky when Hiro, Aya, and Yoshi left the inn. They took a few steps toward the market and then stopped in their tracks.

Kenta and Kazuki were walking toward them!

"There you are, little brother," Kenta said. "Good thing we caught up to you."

"What are you doing here?" Hiro asked as he rushed toward them. "Are you better? And how did you get here so fast?" he asked.

"We don't need as much rest as old Mr. Sato," Kazuki explained. "We got better right after you left. Dad wants you all to come back home right away. He said you should give me the amulet."

Hiro had almost forgotten about the Amulet of the Moon, stashed safely inside his pack.

"Of course," he said. He took off his pack and began to flip through it. He would be glad to get rid of the responsibility.

Hiro's hands found the wooden box that held the amulet. As he took it out, rays of moonlight shone on the carved vessel. Each side of the box showed a different phase of the moon: the waxing moon, the full moon, the waning moon, and the dark moon. Hiro held it out to Kazuki.

"I kept it safe," Hiro said.

Suddenly, Hiro heard Mr. Sato cry out behind him.

"Hiro! No! Don't give it to him!"

Chapter Five

As Kazuki lunged for the box, Hiro snapped out
of his confusion and flipped backward, avoiding his
brother just in time.

"These are not your brothers!" Mr. Sato called
out.

Hiro's mind was spinning. How could that be?
Kazuki and Kenta were standing right in front of
him.

"The old man doesn't know what he's talking

about," Kazuki said. "Now, be a good boy and give me the box."

That was when Hiro noticed Kazuki's eyes. In the moonlight, they glittered a brilliant green instead of their usual pale blue. Mr. Sato was right.

Hiro held the box to his chest. "I don't think so."

Kazuki and Kenta both snarled. They jumped toward Hiro at the same time. Hiro somersaulted across the square to avoid them. He jumped to his feet and couldn't believe what he saw next.

One second earlier, Kazuki and Kenta had looked like his brothers. But now the two creatures staring at Hiro transformed into two sleek black cats with wicked green eyes. They stood on their hind legs, hissing at Hiro.

"They are *bakeneko*," Mr. Sato explained. "Shape-shifting cats. Tricksters."

"I bet they can do some nasty tricks with those claws of theirs," Yoshi cautioned.

"Nice kitties," Hiro said, slowly backing up toward Aya and Yoshi.

"I think they brought some friends with them," Yoshi said nervously.

Hiro glanced around the village square. Four pairs of sinister green eyes glinted in the darkness. Seconds later, four cats stepped out of the shadows, surrounding Hiro.

"What do we do?" Yoshi asked.

"We get back to the inn," Hiro said firmly. "I'm not going to let a bunch of barn cats steal my family's amulet."

The cats lunged at Hiro all at once, knocking him to the ground. He instinctively rolled over to keep his face safe from the cats' sharp claws.

Hiro pushed off the ground and jumped straight up, knocking the cats off him. They tumbled backward, then quickly surrounded the friends, standing on their hind legs once more. The way they stood there made them look more human than cat.

The cats howled and leapt at Hiro. He jumped over them and somersaulted across the square, panting. The cats spun around and bounded toward him.

Before he could dodge them, they slammed into him and knocked him down again.

The box slipped out of Hiro's hand. He quickly rolled on top of it. The cats scrambled onto his back, their claws tearing at his tunic.

Then Hiro heard the cats shriek. They scrambled off him. Hiro rolled over in time to see Aya slithering across the dusty village square. The cats were terrified.

Yoshi ran at all the cats from behind, carrying a bucket of water.

Splash! He dumped the water on all six cats. They yowled and ran away.

"Well done, everyone," Mr. Sato told them as Aya changed back into her usual form.

"That was a good idea about the water, sensei," Yoshi said.

"And you performed the task well," Mr. Sato told him. "Much faster than I would have done."

Hiro cast a nervous glance down the road. "We should get out of this village."

Mr. Sato shook his head. "We are safer in the inn. The bakeneko are most powerful at night. And the swamp is even more dangerous in the dark."

They all went back inside and headed to their room, where they ate a meal of bread and cheese from their packs.

"So much for carrots," Yoshi grumbled.

As they ate, they talked about the strange attack.

"So does this mean the bakeneko are after the Amulet of the Moon?" Hiro asked Mr. Sato.

"Most likely someone is using the bakeneko to try to steal the amulet from you," the teacher replied. "The bakeneko normally steal jewels or other shiny trinkets. But they were looking for the amulet specifically. This is bigger than the bakeneko."

"Could the person controlling them be Fujita?" Aya asked.

"Perhaps," Mr. Sato said. "I do not know. I hope we will find the answers we need at the monastery."

They all washed up and climbed into bed, tired

from the day's journey. Hiro put the wooden box back into his pack and clutched it as he lay down.

But he didn't sleep very well. None of them did.

The sound of wailing cats pacing back and forth outside the inn made sure of that.

Chapter Six

There was no sign of the bakeneko the next morning. Hiro was exhausted, but knowing how close to the monastery they were now propelled him out of bed.

They stopped at the market on their way out of the village, and now Yoshi was happily crunching on carrots as they walked toward Daku Swamp.

"It was pretty cool when you turned into a snake last night, Aya," he said between bites. "It's a good thing cats are scared of snakes. I can't think of anything that is afraid of rabbits."

"You were pretty cool yourself, moving fast like that to throw water on them," Hiro told his friend.

Yoshi grinned. "Yeah, that *was* pretty cool!"

"You all did well," Mr. Sato said. "I am proud to call you my students."

It was nice to get such a compliment from a legendary ninja. But Hiro kept thinking about what Mr. Sato had said the night before—that someone bigger was behind the attempt to steal the amulet. "So far we've just had to fight off some angry cats. What if we have to fight something worse?"

Mr. Sato smiled gently. "We will not know until it happens, will we?" he asked.

Fluffy clouds floated overhead in the blue sky as they walked through the villages. They reached Daku Swamp before noon. As they neared it, Hiro could feel the ground squish underneath his feet.

Tall trees grew out of the murky swamp water. Hiro thought they looked sad. The branches hung down, their mossy green leaves drooping instead of reaching for the sky.

Mr. Sato led them to a small rowboat tied to a post on the edge of the swamp.

"The swamp water is deep in places," he explained. "This is the safest way to cross. Hiro, hold tightly to the amulet. Aya and Yoshi can row."

They climbed inside the boat. Hiro sat in the front and Mr. Sato took the back. Aya and Yoshi sat in the middle and each grabbed an oar.

They slowly glided across the swamp. The towering trees blocked out the sun, so it almost looked like night had fallen early. Hiro shivered, remembering the bakeneko cats and their nighttime tricks, and gripped the pack tightly.

It wasn't easy maneuvering around the trees, but Aya and Yoshi did their best. Something about the swamp kept them all silent.

Hiro slowly realized that the swamp was eerily quiet. There were no frogs croaking, no fish splashing in the water, no birds chattering in the trees.

It's not natural, Hiro thought. *I'll be glad when we get out of here.*

Hiro kept watch from his position in the boat, looking for any sign of danger—or even any sign of life. They had almost reached the swamp's edge when Hiro noticed a patch of dark water churning in front of them.

Hiro put his finger to his lips and motioned for Aya and Yoshi to stop. They set down their oars, giving Hiro a puzzled look.

RAWWWWR!

Something suddenly shot up out of the water in front of them. The looming creature stood on two legs, swamp water dripping from the leathery shell on its back. A ring of stringy black hair surrounded a bowl-shaped indentation on the top of its head. And its green scaly face framed a flat, rubbery beak that was pointed right at the rowboat.

"It's a *kappa!*" Aya yelled.

Every child in the kingdom had grown up hearing stories about monsters called kappa, which lived in rivers, lakes, and swamps. They loved to eat cucumbers—and when there were no cucumbers around, small children would do.

Yoshi started frantically rowing, trying to turn the boat around. The kappa stared at them with large muddy brown eyes, as if it was deciding its next move.

Hiro tried to remember the tales he'd heard as a young kid. There was water in the bowl on the kappa's head. The water was the source of the kappa's power. If you tricked the kappa into spilling the water, you could escape.

Hiro stood up and closed his eyes.

"Monkey power!" he yelled.

Hiro jumped up and transformed in midair. He grabbed a low-hanging tree branch with his monkey hand and swung right in front of the kappa's face.

"Betcha can't catch me!" Hiro taunted.

The kappa roared and stomped toward Hiro, splashing swamp water all around it. But it kept its head straight, not spilling a drop of water from the top.

Hiro knew he would somehow have to get the kappa to bend over. He swung to another tree branch. The kappa reached out with two long arms and slimy webbed hands.

Hiro somersaulted off the branch, falling into the water in front of the kappa. The creature bent down to grab him, just as Hiro had hoped.

Sparkling green water splashed out of the bowl on the kappa's head.

RAWWWWR! The creature angrily grabbed the sides of its head and slid back under the water.

Satisfied, Hiro climbed back into the boat.

"Quick thinking, Hiro. You did well," Mr. Sato said. "And now I suggest we make our way out of the swamp as quickly as possible."

Aya and Yoshi didn't need any prodding. They rowed as fast as they could until they came to a small dock. Aya climbed out of the boat first and anchored it to the dock with a long strand of rope.

Yoshi jumped out behind Aya. "That was scary!" he said. "But what happened to the kappa?"

"It's like in the stories, remember?" Aya said. "Hiro tricked the kappa into spilling the water on top of its head. That's how the kappa loses its power. Hiro saved us."

Hiro felt himself blush. "Come on. We'd better find the Monks of the Dusk."

Yoshi nodded toward the end of the dock. "Uh, I think they found us."

A boy in a dark blue robe stood there, smiling at them. His hair was shaved closely to his head.

"The Monks of the Dusk welcome you," he said.

Chapter Seven

The boy bowed. "My name is Akio. We sensed that visitors were approaching and might be in danger. But I see you and your monkey have passed safely through the swamp."

Hiro remembered he was still in his monkey form. He concentrated for a minute and then changed back. Akio's dark eyes widened.

"I am very sorry," he said, bowing again. "I did not realize you were a ninja in fighting form."

"It's okay," Hiro replied, smiling. "I don't mind being mistaken for a monkey. It's part of who I am. My name is Hiro. These are my friends Aya and Yoshi, and our teacher, Mr. Sato."

"Welcome," Akio repeated.

"Thank you," Mr. Sato replied. "This is not the first time I have visited your monastery. I am looking forward to seeing my old friend Master Kazuo."

A troubled look crossed Akio's face. But it was gone so quickly Hiro wasn't sure he'd seen it in the first place.

"Please, follow me," Akio said.

The group trailed after Akio down a path thickly lined with curling vines and dense vegetation. Hiro was beginning to wonder how far away the monastery was when it suddenly rose out of the undergrowth before them.

They stood in the shadow of a large four-story stone tower topped with sloping eaves. On each tier of the tower, one of the phases of the moon was carved. A full moon had been carved

into the top layer of the temple.

Just like the box that holds the Amulet of the Moon! thought Hiro.

Akio pushed open the dark wood doors of the tower and they stepped into a wide entry hall. Polished wood planks lined the floor, and rice paper screens covered the wide windows. A small stone fountain bubbled in the center of the space.

A door on the far wall slid open, and a group of monks in blue robes entered to greet them. Most of the monks had shaved heads, like Akio, and walked with their eyes facing the floor. But their leader had wavy black hair and a long, curved mustache.

"Welcome, visitors," he said cheerfully. "I am Mareo, leader of the Monks of the Dusk."

Mr. Sato stepped forward and bowed. "Respectfully, Master," he said, "I thought that Kazuo was the leader of this monastery."

Mareo's green eyes flashed for a moment. Then he bowed his head. "I am sorry to be the bearer of bad news, but Kazuo has died," the monk said. "He appointed me as his successor."

Mr. Sato took the news calmly. "I understand," he said. Then he walked to stand behind Hiro, Aya, and Yoshi.

Hiro was worried. What if Kazuo was the only one who could have helped them? He opened his pack and took out the box holding the Amulet of the Moon. All eyes in the room turned to the box, which looked like it held something important.

"My name is Hiro Hinata, from Hissori Village," he said. "My family guards the Amulet of the Moon. But during the full moon, my mother and brothers came down with some kind of sickness. Mr. Sato thought you might be able to help us."

Hiro turned to Mr. Sato, but he wasn't there. Puzzled, Hiro looked around the room. "Mr. Sato?"

"That's weird," Yoshi said. "He was right here."

"Perhaps he was overcome by grief," Mareo suggested. "I will send my monks to find him."

He held out his hand. "In the meantime, I can help you. May I see the amulet?"

It wasn't easy for Hiro to hand over the amulet to a stranger, but that was why they had traveled all this way, wasn't it? He carefully put the box in Mareo's hands.

The monk's green eyes glittered as he opened the lid.

"It's mine!" he said. Then he turned to the monks behind him. "Take them!"

Before Hiro, Aya, and Yoshi could react, the monks swarmed them, grabbing them by the arms. Hiro looked at Akio, who was standing against the wall. He avoided Hiro's gaze.

"What's going on?" Hiro asked.

Mareo smiled, but it was a sinister smile, not the fake cheerful one he had worn before.

"You have brought me the object I desire, and now I have no need of you," Mareo replied. "Men! Throw them in the prison!"

Chapter Eight

"It was all a trick," Hiro said glumly.

He leaned back against the cold stone wall of the underground prison cell he shared with Aya and Yoshi. A grate of metal bars locked them inside.

"I don't understand," Yoshi said. "How did they know we were coming with the amulet? And where's Mr. Sato?"

Aya sat in the corner of the cell with an angry look on her face.

"I can't believe we got captured," she muttered. "I should have transformed into a snake and fought them."

"That would not have been wise." Akio stood outside the cell. "You could not have fought them all. At least you are safe here," he said.

"What do you want?" Hiro snapped.

Akio knelt down. "We do not have much time. The guard will soon return. I am sorry you are here."

"Then why'd you let them do it?" Yoshi asked.

"It is Mareo," Akio explained. "Kazuo is not dead. He is a prisoner, like you. Mareo came one night with his bakeneko. They do his bidding, stealing things for him and attacking his enemies. He is a monk, but an evil one, with ties to Fujita, who—"

"We know all about Fujita," Hiro interrupted him. "We've fought him before."

Akio looked surprised. "Then maybe you do not need my help."

Yoshi jumped to his feet. "Oh, we need all the help we can get. Can you get us out of here?"

"You must escape from the cell on your own, but if you do, I can lead you safely away from the monastery," Akio told them.

"I still don't understand," Hiro said. "Why are the monks helping Mareo?"

Akio looked down. "I am ashamed to say it, but we are afraid of him. He has threatened to harm our families if we disobey him. And some of the monks, like your guard, have turned to Mareo's side. They are fooled by his promises of power and riches."

There was a noise down the hall, and Akio quickly stood. "Go up the staircase on the left. That leads to the kitchen. The cook is not loyal to Mareo and will let you pass."

The guard appeared seconds after Akio left them. A brass key hung from a sash around the guard's waist. He walked over to a wood bench across from the cell and sat there, a bored look on his face. The key dangled over the side of the bench.

"Distract the guard," Aya hissed. "I'll get the key."

Hiro and Yoshi nodded. They stood side by side, blocking the guard's view of Aya. She quickly transformed into a snake and quietly slid across the floor of the cell, through the bars.

"I'll do it," Yoshi whispered in Hiro's ear.

Then he called out. "Hey! Guard! When's dinner?"

The guard snickered. "You'll eat when Mareo says you can eat," he said, laughing.

As he talked, Aya gripped the key in her mouth and tried to slide it off the sash, but she couldn't get past the knot. She gave the sash a tug, hoping it would come loose.

The guard felt the pull, and Hiro's heart jumped as the monk looked down and saw Aya there. She was caught.

"Aaaaah! A snake!" the monk screamed. He jumped off the bench, and the sash slid off his waist. He ran down the hall as fast as he could.

Hiro breathed a sigh of relief. "Good thing he was afraid of snakes," he said. "Quick! Let's get out of here!"

Aya's body shimmered with green light and she changed into her human form.

"Striking fear in the hearts of my enemies is turning out to be a pretty good thing," she said, grinning. She put the key into the lock and opened the door.

Yoshi ran ahead of them. "Akio said to use the left staircase," he said.

But Hiro stopped. Yoshi frowned, puzzled. "Come on, we have to hurry!"

"Hurry to do what?" Hiro asked. "Escape, and leave Mr. Sato and the amulet behind? I can't do that."

"We could go for help," Yoshi suggested.

"From who, the kappa monster?" Hiro shook his head. "We've got to find Mareo and get that amulet back."

"Of course," Aya said. "So where do we find him?"

Hiro remembered the moon carvings outside the temple. He knew that the full moon was thought to hold the most power of all of the moon's phases. A greedy monk like Mareo would probably want all the power he could get.

Hiro pointed to the staircase on the right. "We're going up to the top of the tower. I bet that's where Mareo is."

"We'll get caught if anyone sees us," Aya warned.

Hiro knew she was right, but there had to be some way to do it. He glanced around the prison area and noticed a blue robe hanging over a hook by the guard's bench.

"This'll work," he said.

"But there's only one," Aya pointed out.

Hiro grinned. "I have an idea."

"Yoshi! Quit wiggling," Hiro said.

"I can't help it," Yoshi replied. "You're squishing me!"

Hiro slowly and steadily walked up the staircase

to the fourth floor of the tower. He wore the guard's blue robe with the hood over his head to cover up his hair. He held Yoshi in rabbit form under the long sleeves of the robe. Aya, in snake form, was curled around his waist like a belt.

"Hurry up!" Aya hissed. "I'm ssstarting to sssslip! I'm not used to clenching my ssssstomach mussssscles like thissss."

"Shhh!" Hiro warned. A monk passed them as he came down the stairs, and Hiro lowered his head so the monk wouldn't see his face.

Finally they reached the top. The staircase opened up to a hallway that held only a huge wood door with a large full moon carved in the center. On each side of the door sat a pillar topped with a small carved statue of a bat.

"This has got to be it," Hiro said. The hall was empty, so he took off the monk's robe. Aya slithered off him, and Yoshi jumped to the ground. Then they both transformed.

"What next?" Aya asked.

Hiro wasn't sure. He didn't even know if Mareo was in there or not. And they couldn't just walk in. . . .

"I don't know," Hiro said. He reached out to touch the door.

BAM!

A powerful blast of white light exploded in the space, throwing Hiro backward. He slammed into the wall and then slid to the floor in a heap.

"Hiro!" Aya yelled.

Chapter Nine

Hiro opened his eyes. He felt a little groggy, but he wasn't hurt.

"Are you all right?" Aya asked.

Hiro slowly stood up. "I think so."

The white light crackled and sparked in front of the door.

"It's some kind of magical barrier," Aya said.

"How are we supposed to get past it?" Yoshi asked.

The friends studied the barrier. It covered every inch of the door.

"I can't even transform and slide under it," Aya said after a minute. "It goes all the way from the floor to the ceiling."

Yoshi sighed. "Too bad we don't know anything about magic."

Magic. That was it!

"But we do," Hiro said. He started tapping his forehead. "Remember? Mr. Sato said this could help us see where magic is coming from."

"I thought he was just tired," Yoshi said.

"Come on!" Hiro urged. "We have to try."

Hiro kept tapping the center of his forehead, just like Mr. Sato had told him to. For a minute, nothing happened. Hiro started to feel a little silly, but he couldn't give up. And then . . .

The sizzling white barrier seemed to fade, and Hiro saw two swirling waves of purple light. They were coming from the carved bats.

"Do you see that?" Hiro asked.

Aya nodded. "Mareo must have charmed the bat carvings to create the barrier," she said. "If we take them down, maybe we can get rid of it."

Hiro studied the bats. They were up high, but each one was just outside the barrier's reach.

He closed his eyes, transforming into a monkey. Then he jumped up and grabbed a wood ceiling beam. He swung to the pillar on the left.

Slam! He knocked the bat off the pillar. It clattered to the floor. Half of the white barrier fizzled out.

Hiro swung to the other side and knocked the other bat off the pillar. The barrier faded.

"All right!" Yoshi cheered. "Let's get the amulet."

"I think you guys should transform again," Hiro said. "Mareo might be expecting three kids to stop him. But he's probably not expecting a monkey, a rabbit, and a snake."

"Good thinking," Aya said. She and Yoshi quickly transformed. Now a monkey, a rabbit, and a snake stood facing the door.

"You'd better open it, Hiro," Aya said. "I don't have any handsssss."

Hiro opened the door and they slowly crept inside. Scrolls cluttered the floor of Mareo's large study. Stones, crystals, and jars filled with strange-looking liquid filled shelves and tabletops. Hiro motioned for them to hide behind a tall bookshelf. As they settled in, they could hear Mareo muttering to himself on the other side of the room.

"Surely a magician of power, such as myself, should be able to wield the amulet," he said, his voice rising with frustration. "Fujita mastered it. There must be some way. . . ."

Hiro peeked out from behind the shelf. Mareo was sitting at a large desk. He was staring at the amulet's box in front of him. Hiro realized with relief that Mareo had not been able to take the amulet out of the box yet.

"I'm going to try to surprise him," Hiro whispered to his friends.

"What if it doesn't work?" Yoshi asked.

Hiro shrugged. "I guess we can figure that out as we go along."

"Hiro, that'ssss no kind of plan," Aya hissed.

But Hiro didn't have any better ideas. He jumped onto Mareo's desk and grabbed the box.

"I'll take that, thanks," Hiro said. He jumped again, grabbed on to a ceiling beam, and swung quickly toward the door.

Mareo sprang from his chair, sputtering in fury.

"Give that back!" he shrieked.

He pointed at Hiro with his right hand. Purple sparks shot from his fingers.

"Hiro, look out!" Yoshi yelled. He hopped toward Hiro, with Aya slithering behind him.

Hiro swung to another beam, narrowly missing a jagged bolt of purple lightning. Mareo turned on him, his face red with anger.

"You cannot escape me!" he yelled.

He pointed at the ceiling beam, and the wood snapped in two. Hiro went tumbling to the floor,

landing on Yoshi and Aya. The sudden crash caused all three to transform back into humans. Mareo towered over them.

"Now to finish it," he said with an evil grin.

Whooosh!

A wave of blue light swept into the room, surrounding Mareo in a bubble. The blue bubble of light carried him to the ceiling.

Hiro got to his feet and looked toward the door. Mr. Sato stood next to a blue-robed monk with a wrinkled face. The old monk's hands were raised, and the blue energy was pouring out of them.

"Kazuo!" Mareo cried. Purple lightning shot from his fingers, but could not get past Kazuo's magic.

Kazuo lowered his head and closed his eyes. The blue wave of light washed over the room. Hiro felt his whole body tingle.

Suddenly, they all stood outside, in front of Daku Swamp. Dusk had fallen, and the round, bright moon was just rising in the east. Mareo hovered above the dark swamp water in his blue bubble.

"Be gone from here, Mareo," Kazuo said. "Be gone, and do not return."

Mareo's eyes gleamed. "This is not over. Bakeneko, I call on you!"

A small army of black bakeneko cats emerged from the trees. Once more, they stood on their hind legs, looking almost human. Several monks from the monastery flanked the cats. Hiro recognized one of them as the prison guard.

These must be the monks loyal to Mareo, he reasoned.

"*Attack!*" Mareo yelled.

Thinking quickly, Hiro, Aya, and Yoshi rushed toward Mr. Sato, forming a circle and keeping their backs to one another so they could defend themselves from all sides.

The bakeneko attacked first, throwing themselves at the ninja, each cat a blur of fur, claws, and snarling teeth. One cat flew toward Hiro, and he grabbed it and tossed it into the water.

The monks attacked next. A young monk ready to

deliver a dangerous kick flew at Hiro, who grabbed the monk's outstretched leg and flipped over it, avoiding the blow. Next to him, Yoshi ducked between the legs of a monk to avoid a punch while Aya flipped forward to kick another monk in the stomach. On his other side, Mr. Sato was sending monk after monk flying with a nimble flick of his walking stick.

They were fighting well, but they were greatly outnumbered. Hiro feared they couldn't last much longer.

Mareo watched, laughing. "You cannot defeat us. You will crumble before us, just like before," he said.

"Not this time."

Hiro turned to see Akio and the other Monks of the Dusk behind them. Many of the monks held fighting staffs. They looked angry.

"This time, we will fight back," Akio said.

The monks let out a mighty cry and charged forward, pulling Mareo's monks off Hiro and the others. Hiro saw the bakeneko he had fought slink out of the water on the border of the fray. He joined the other cats, and they all disappeared into the darkness.

"Noooooo!" Mareo wailed.

Kazuo lifted his arms high in the air. Mareo floated higher and higher above the swamp. Then the bubble burst, and Mareo was gone.

"It is over," Kazuo said. For the first time, he looked at Hiro. "And now, young man, I believe we have a problem to discuss."

Chapter Ten

Kazuo led them back inside the monastery.

"Mareo said you were dead," Yoshi piped up.

Kazuo smiled. "As you can see, I am not," he said. "I was imprisoned, and my old friend Okuno freed me."

He put his hands together and bowed to Mr. Sato. "Thank you, friend. And now please let me help you."

"It's my mother and brothers," Hiro said. "One minute they were fine, and the next minute, they were asleep and wouldn't wake up. They all used the

Amulet of the Moon. Did that hurt them somehow?"

Kazuo shook his head. "I don't believe so," he said. "It sounds more like shadow sickness."

"What's that?" Yoshi asked.

"When someone's shadow is stolen by magic, they fall into a deep sleep," Kazuo replied. "They cannot wake until the shadow is restored."

Hiro nodded, remembering. "That has to be it! When we were at Mrs. Sasaki's house, I saw a kitten playing with Kenta's and Kazuki's shadows. Then it looked like the shadows disappeared. I thought it was weird."

"That kitten was likely a bakeneko," Kazuo said. "Then my suspicion is confirmed. That is good. I know a potion that can restore a lost shadow. I will prepare some for you to take back to your family."

A wave of relief swept over Hiro.

"Thank you so much," he said.

"So are you saying that Mareo sent the bakeneko to steal the shadows?" Aya asked.

Kazuo looked at Mr. Sato, who nodded. "I think

I can put together the pieces of this puzzle," their teacher said. "Shadow sickness is just one of the tricks the bakeneko use to torment humans. I should have realized this when we first encountered them. Mareo must have sent them to Hissori to steal the shadows of Rino, Kenta, and Kazuki. Because of the full moon, he knew we would connect their illness to the amulet and seek help from the Monks of the Dusk. And just as he had hoped, we brought the amulet right to him."

Hiro couldn't believe it. "So the whole thing was a big trick to get the amulet." He looked down at the box. "If Mareo would go to so much trouble to get it, what else can happen?"

Akio stepped forward. "Hiro, I am sorry we put you and your friends in danger. If you ever need help, the Monks of the Dusk are here for you."

"Thank you," Hiro replied, smiling at his new friend. "And if *you* ever need help, just send a message to Hissori Village."

It took several hours for Kazuo to prepare the

cure. Hiro kept both the Amulet of the Moon and the glass vial containing the elixir safe in his pack the whole way home.

Rino, Kenta, and Kazuki were counting on him.

〰〰〰

"So I've been asleep for a week?" Kenta asked, yawning.

"Impossible," Kazuki said. "I'm still tired."

Rino reached out and hugged Hiro. "I am so glad you got home safely!"

Rino and Yuto's room was very crowded. Rino, Kenta, and Kazuki sat up in bed. They had woken up shortly after being given Kazuo's cure. Hiro's family listened as he told the story of their journey, with some help from Aya, Yoshi, and Mr. Sato.

"I can't believe you saw a kappa," Kenta said. "I used to have nightmares about those when I was a kid."

"It wasn't so bad," Hiro said, shrugging. It felt good to show off a little bit in front of his brothers.

"Speak for yourself," Yoshi said. "I hope I never see another one as long as I live!"

Everyone laughed.

"I must be going," Mr. Sato said. "It has been a long journey, and I need to rest my old bones."

"Wait, Mr. Sato," Hiro said. Something had been bothering him. He knew if he didn't ask about it now, he might never ask. "I need to know. Why did you disappear right before Mareo captured us?"

"That is a very good question," Mr. Sato said. "When Mareo told me Kazuo was dead, I knew he was lying. And I also knew he must be very powerful. It would take powerful magic to imprison a monk like Kazuo. Finding him was our only hope."

"I understand," Hiro said. But he still felt a little bit hurt. It bothered him that Mr. Sato had left them alone to deal with Mareo.

Mr. Sato saw the look on Hiro's face. "I would never have left you if I had not had faith in you," he said gently. "I knew you and Aya and Yoshi could take care of yourselves. And you did."

Hiro immediately felt better. "Thank you," he said.

Mr. Sato left. Aya looked at Yoshi. "We should go, too," she said. "I'm sure Hiro wants to be with his family."

"Sure," Yoshi said. He rubbed his stomach. "I'm hungry, anyway."

"I'll walk you out," Hiro offered.

They stepped outside into the night. The waning moon was a curved shape in the sky now, but still very bright.

Yoshi looked from side to side.

"Just checking for weird cats," he said.

"I don't think we have to worry about them anymore," Aya told him.

"Probably not," Hiro agreed. "But we should always be on guard. Fujita's evil is spreading across the kingdom like a plague. I don't want to be tricked again."

Aya nodded. "You're right. But don't worry, Hiro. We're with you."

She put her right hand on top of Hiro's. Yoshi slapped his hand on top of hers.

"Oh, yeah! We're ready!" Yoshi cheered.

Hiro smiled. With the help of his friends, he felt like he could do anything.

HIRO'S WORLD

Hiro's Quest is a work of fantasy, but it is based on some real ideas and elements from Japan and other places around the world.

Good Cats, Bad Cats
A Note from the Author

Many cultures associate cats with magic and the moon. Some lore treats cats with suspicion, like the old superstition that if a black cat crosses your path, you'll have bad luck.

Stories of cats being able to transform into humans are quite common. In Japan, these cats are called *bakeneko* or *neko-mata*. Legends say these cats may cause people to get sick or start fires. In *The Shadow Stealers*, I changed the bakeneko and made them thieves with the magical ability to steal shadows.

Not all legends portray cats as nasty creatures. If you've ever been in a Chinese restaurant, you might have seen a statue of a *Maneki Neko*, a smiling white cat with one paw raised in the air. These statues are thought to be good luck charms that will bring money or customers into a business.

Of course, whether you believe in legends or not, you can always enjoy cats as loving and special pets. My cat, Katie, likes to sit on my desk as I write. I don't know if she is a Maneki Neko, but I like to think she brings me good luck!

Get a sneak peek at the next exciting chapter in

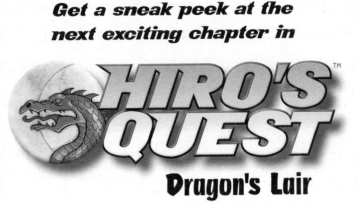

HIRO'S QUEST ™

Dragon's Lair

The nine days of travel had passed slowly for Hiro. He was anxious to get to Gado Village and find the dragon. Along the way, he'd seen many interesting sights: strange flowers the color of the rising sun, rocks that looked like sleeping monsters, a swimming hole that looked impossibly deep and cool. But Hiro was always thinking about the adventure ahead.

And now they were finally here. Gado Village was surrounded by thick woods on three sides. The wooden cottages looked similar to the homes in Hissori Village, although the land was flat instead of sloped and steep. Mr. Kigi led them to a pleasant-looking cottage with a grove of berry bushes in front and a wire pen on the side, occupied by one peaceful cow. As they approached, the door flew open and a woman ran outside, followed by three children.

"Benjiro, you're home!" she cried. She and the children threw their arms around him, practically knocking him to the ground.

Mr. Kigi laughed. "I have missed you so!" he said. He picked up the youngest child, a chubby boy who looked about three years old. "Have you been a good boy?"

"Yes, papa," the boy said.

"I traveled far to find ninja who will search for the dragon," he said. "Please welcome our guests."

Mr. Kigi's family hadn't noticed Hiro and the others before; now they stared at them, wide-eyed.

"Are you really ninja?" asked the oldest, a girl.

Hiro nodded. "I am Hiro Hinata, and these are my friends Aya and Yoshi, and our *sensei*, Mr. Sato."

Mrs. Kigi bowed. "Welcome to our home," she said. "You must share our supper."

They followed her into a room with a long wood

dining table. Mrs. Kigi quickly set the table with plates and bowls. She couldn't have known they were coming yet there was enough bread and soup for all of them—including Yoshi, who had thirds of everything.

When the meal was finished, they all helped to clear the table.

"The sun is setting," Mrs. Kigi said. "I will set up sleeping quarters for you."

"There will be no need," said Mr. Sato, standing up. "Mr. Kigi has told us that the dragon has been often spotted at night. We must begin our search."

"Really?" Hiro asked, surprised. "We don't have to wait until tomorrow?"

"You have traveled such a long way," Mrs. Kigi said. "Surely you need some rest."

Aya yawned at the mention of the word "rest." But Mr. Sato was not swayed. Hiro thought he seemed unusually excited.

"Thank you for your hospitality," Mr. Sato said. "We will return when we have news to report."

The sky was streaked with orange as they headed

into the forest. They didn't get far before the trees seemed to close in around them. It was difficult to see in the dim light, and Hiro knew soon it would get even darker.

"Mr. Sato, we didn't bring any lanterns," Hiro said.

"If we had lanterns, the dragon would see us and hide," the teacher responded. "Our eyes will adjust to the darkness well enough to see our way."

"But it will be difficult to spot the dragon in the dark," Aya pointed out.

Mr. Sato nodded at her. "You know what to do."

Aya closed her eyes and concentrated. Then a shimmering green light surrounded her body. She transformed into a snake with shiny green scales.

"I have excellent night vision," she said. "It comessss with being a sssssnake."

"Cool!" Yoshi said.

"Ssssomebody should pick me up," Aya said. "Then I can lead the way."

Hiro picked up Aya. She wrapped her long body around his arms.

"Thanksss, Hiro."

"No problem," Hiro replied.

They quietly made their way through the forest. Aya warned them about low-hanging tree branches and rocks.

"So we're just supposed to walk around until we find the dragon?" Yoshi asked after a while, in a loud whisper.

"We are heading east, toward the lake," Mr. Sato replied. "I believe that is where we will find her."

Her. So Mr. Sato thought the dragon was female. Hiro wanted to ask him about it, but knew he'd only receive some mysterious answer.

He was still lost in thought when he heard Aya cry out.

"Hiro, look out!"

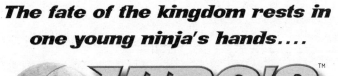